Honey and the Chickens

The Orchard Escapade

by L J Glasgow

Illustrated by Lisa Williams

Honey and the Chickens
The Orchard Escapade

By L J Glasgow

Illustrated by Lisa Williams

First published in 2022

ISBN: 978-1-7391891-0-5

For James, Dominic and William.

But I mustn't forget my inspirations: Honey, Tulip, Rose, Daisy and Blossom, as they do actually exist!

Thank you.

Contents

Oh, what a glorious day

The warmth from the sun was particularly satisfying today, and Honey was enjoying lying out on the patio, lapping up the heat from its far-reaching rays. Her hooman was happily dozing in the deckchair beside her and was in no particular rush to move from this sunny spot. As she stretched and rolled onto her back, she could feel the heat working its way up from the tips of her paws to the end of her shiny black nose. She let out a sigh, allowing the feeling of happiness and contentment engulf her. This was going to be a good day. She could just tell.

As Honey lay stretched out on the patio, daydreaming and watching a solitary, fluffy, white cloud tiptoe across the sky, she suddenly became very aware of an incredibly loud clucking sound coming from the top of the garden. Her friends, the chickens, were trying their very best to get her attention. So she

enjoyed one last stretch before trotting up the garden to the chicken coop to see them.

"Good morning, ladies!" Honey called to them. "Are you enjoying this wonderful day?"

"Shush, Honey. Keep your voice down! We don't want the hoomans to hear us," said Tulip sternly.

Now this confused Honey, considering the chickens only moments ago were clucking as if they were in a big brass band. But she didn't feel it was appropriate at this time to point this out to Tulip, as she was intrigued to hear what was so important that they had to disturb her sunbathing. Her hooman, who was now snoring in his deckchair, seemed oblivious to all the commotion.

Tulip stepped forward and nodded at Honey, suggesting she meet her at the door of their coop, which their hooman had left slightly ajar that morning. Tulip was the unofficial leader of the group. She had not been voted by any of the others but was the eldest, and her bossy nature had made her the more natural fit for the role.

Some would say the coop was a very lavish space for four average-sized chickens. However, the chickens were keen explorers and often liked to plan great adventures away from it. Honey walked towards the door, where she was met by a very excited Tulip, who could not wait to tell her about today's planned adventure.

"Now, Honey, are you listening carefully?" whispered Tulip, who didn't actually wait to hear Honey's response before continuing. "Magpie recently told Robin, who then mentioned it to Sparrow, who then told Rose at breakfast this morning," Tulip quickly rattled off, without coming up for breath, "that beyond the hedge is an apple orchard, which has apples galore. Far more apples than any hooman could possibly desire."

Honey already knew of these orchards as she had often enjoyed walking in them with her hoomans. The quaint and picturesque village where Honey and the chickens lived stood proudly on a hill overlooking a sea of green fields and woodlands. It was only made more idyllic by the vast orchards surrounding it, which many hoomans walked around appreciating their natural beauty and breathtaking landscape which framed them. Honey was picturing herself surrounded by apples, eating as many as she could devour, when an impatient cluckity-cluck sound put an immediate end to her daydreaming.

"I am sorry, Tulip. What were you saying?"

"Oh really, Honey, you must try to keep up. This is going to be one of our best adventures yet!"

Rose, Blossom and Daisy joined them at the door, nodding and clucking enthusiastically.

"It really is, Honey. Just wait and see." Rose grinned, feeling confident about such things and a keen supporter of anything adventurous. She would always wholeheartedly agree to any of Tulip's ideas, however risky they may be.

The only problem with the chickens' so-called 'great ideas', were that they often required Honey to get involved and sometimes save them from getting into all sorts of difficulties. There was that one occasion when Tulip got trapped in the very prickly bush. She believed it was only prickly because it was guarding something amazing. However, she quickly discovered there was most definitely nothing amazing in the bush and that she was now stuck and unable to get out. If it weren't for Honey alerting the hoomans and showing them where Tulip was, she would have been stuck in there forever.

The chickens' new plan involved sneaking out of the coop, crossing the garden and over the hedge before making their way across a playing field (which was greatly enjoyed by hoomans and their dogs) and entering the gate to the orchard where they could feast on the apples.

Now some may think this would be quite a straightforward plan, but Blossom had recently been enjoying far more food than any of the others, and she had become quite plump. This would definitely stop her from being able to sprint the distance, if needed, without taking a rest half-way. It would also obviously make them very easy to spot, and no doubt any hoomans walking their dogs at the time would alert the chickens' hooman, and they would be immediately returned to their coop, and their adventure would come to an abrupt end. This really wouldn't do! So another route had to be found, and that's where Honey could help.

Honey, like most other dogs, often took her hoomans for a daily walk. It is certainly not the other way around like most hoomans would let you believe. Dogs are fully aware that hoomans must have regular exercise, which is good for their health and well-being.

So Honey had often walked in the orchards and knew another route, away from hoomans, the chickens could try. It would involve going through the allotment that sat next to the coop, crawling under the fence into their neighbour's garden (a route Hattie hedgehog and her children often used), before hopping over the small wall into the church's garden. With all its trees and bushes, the church's garden would allow them to zigzag their way unnoticed across to the orchard, which sat next to the church. The chickens loved this plan and were more than willing to give it a go. What could possibly go wrong?

Let the adventure begin

So the chickens each went to a corner of their coop to check that the coast was clear. They all looked left and then right. The male hooman was still fast asleep in his deckchair, and the female hooman was nowhere to be seen. It was now or never! With Honey's help, they pushed the already slightly ajar door open. Then in single file, with Tulip leading the way, they ran from the coop to the allotment, with Honey trotting behind at the back.

As they made their way across the allotment to the fence, Blossom couldn't resist pecking at the courgettes which the hoomans were successfully growing. *They look so enticing, and I am sure the hoomans wouldn't notice if a little one went missing*, thought Blossom.

"Oh really, Blossom, this is no time to be thinking about your stomach," snapped Daisy, who often felt quite anxious on their adventures.

She always preferred to stick to the plan and did not like it when others didn't. It made her start to panic.

"But Daisy, it is just a little snack," moaned Blossom, her cheeks bulging with courgette. "It might be ages before I get to eat again."

"No, Blossom! Step away from the courgettes," ordered Tulip. "We can't afford to waste any time!"

Daisy was relieved that Tulip had taken control of the situation, and they could now continue with the plan.

Blossom reluctantly started to back away from the courgettes, but as the others turned away and headed to the fence, she took one last sneaky mouthful just to keep her going and to stop her tummy rumbling.

Tulip was first to go under the fence, followed by Daisy, then Rose, who was more than ready to take on the challenge of this new adventure. Rose particularly loved the adrenalin rush of a tricky challenge and, even more so, the warm fuzzy feeling you have when you successfully complete a challenge.

When it came to Blossom's turn, she found that the recent months of overindulgence had caused her to get stuck under the fence, which was highly embarrassing and no doubt not something her sisters would ever let her forget. Unfortunately, there was only one thing for it, Honey had to give her a push in the hope that it would release her from her predicament, but she could see that this wouldn't be easy, as Blossom was well and truly stuck. She would have to take a run up and give her an extremely hard push.

Honey backed away, and on the count of three, she ran as fast as she could towards Blossom's big feathery bottom. With an almighty push, Blossom burst through the gap and landed awkwardly at her sisters' feet. Acting as if nothing had happened, Blossom stood up and patted her now very ruffled feathers down and decided to ignore her three sisters' glares of annoyance.

Honey was now on her own, having to make a tough decision. Should she go under the fence and risk getting stuck like Blossom, or should she try jumping over it? How hard could that be? She had seen her friend, Major the sheepdog, jump high up onto the back of his owner's tractor many times. Surely, she could jump over a fence. But the fence was high, and it towered over her. Nervously Honey took twenty paces back before sprinting as fast as she could towards it. Then with one almighty leap, she cleared the fence and landed very gracefully at Rose's feet.

"Oh well done, Honey!" the chickens clucked. "Superbly done!"

Honey, who was grinning from ear to ear, took a bow. She was very proud of her achievement, so much so that she decided never to doubt herself again because she now knew with a little bit of confidence, anything could be achieved.

"Right, ladies, time is rapidly passing us by. We need to complete this adventure and get home before the hoomans discover we are missing. Let's run to the wall!" ordered Tulip.

Blossom wasn't overly keen on the idea of running and made it a habit not to run unless it was life-saving, but she knew there was a great reward waiting on this particular occasion. Honey and her sisters were carefully checking that the path was clear, so had not noticed Blossom lifting her feathers away from her legs so that she could move more freely. Mustering all her courage, she began to run towards the wall. The chickens and Honey did a double take. They were astonished at how quickly Blossom could actually run, as it was such a rare sight. *It's amazing what you can achieve with a little motivation,* thought Honey.

They all quickly sped after her before taking a few minutes by the wall to catch their breath. Once they had all controlled their breathing and were not huffing and puffing like mini steam trains, they all hopped one by one over the wall into the church's garden. Thankfully, they landed behind a big yew bush. The yew bushes' dense, green foliage provided the perfect hiding spot. This now allowed them to safely work out their next move.

The sun was climbing quite high in the now cloudless, blue sky, and they were all starting to feel quite hot and bothered, especially after so much excitement. A bead of sweat trickled down Rose's beak and plopped onto the dust below her. To their relief, the yew bush provided some much-needed shade, which the chickens welcomed with open wings and allowed them to appreciate the coolness—it was heavenly!

Luckily, it didn't take long for them to feel recharged and ready for their next manoeuvre. The orchard was now in sight.

They were just moments away from enjoying those big red juicy apples.

Time for a little faith

Now the only problem with going via the church garden is the risk of being spotted by one of the church's volunteers, who regularly tend the garden to make it a more tranquil place for all who visit it. This was one detail Honey had forgotten to mention to the chickens. It didn't seem relevant at the time, as she had never considered the volunteers a threat before. In fact, Honey often liked to say hello to them when she was out walking her hoomans. But for the chickens, being spotted by a volunteer would mean the adventure would be over before it had really begun.

On this particular occasion, there was a volunteer mowing the grass. It was Les, a very friendly hooman who often liked to pat Honey on the head and give her a treat. *I wonder if I should just quickly say hello*, thought Honey, now thinking about her stomach. *He may have a treat for me, and I really do love a treat.*

No, I must not! Honey scolded herself. *My friends need me to help them. I must remain focused!* Honey's deliberation was suddenly interrupted by someone calling her name.

"Honey, Honey, what do we do now?" a very anxious Daisy asked, as things were clearly not going to plan. She could feel the little ball of worry that was always there when carrying out these adventures but was usually tucked away in a corner of her stomach. But now it was starting to grow rapidly. She began to feel quite sick with nerves.

Taking one look at Daisy's very worried face, Honey knew she now had to find the best route to stop them from bumping into Les and potentially ruining their adventure. She peered through the branches of the yew bush and could see that Les had his back to them and was mowing the main lawn in front of the church. Honey carefully watched him. He appeared to be creating patterns on the lawn. They looked like lines. This was something her hoomans liked to do in their garden too. She couldn't see the point herself, but she always found it quite fascinating to watch. She so enjoyed the smell of cut grass but not as much as rolling around on it. That was just the best feeling. Although oddly enough, her hoomans were not so keen on her doing this, as admittedly, her fur changed from a beautiful creamy colour to green. But does that really warrant having to have a bath? Honey didn't think so and thought it was a little extreme.

Les was getting nearer to the church, and Honey could see that he would turn around, which meant that he would soon be mowing the grass towards them. They had to act fast! They must now run to the gate and into the orchard whilst Les couldn't see them.

"Ladies, we need to run now!" shouted Honey over the noise of the lawn mower.

The chickens nervously looked at each other but agreed to follow Honey on her say-so.

Honey took one last look, then bellowed,
"READY, STEADY, GO!"

There was no time for a single file this time.
They just had to run, and run as fast as their
little chicken legs could carry them. With their
tail feathers flapping in the wind, they ran and
ran and ran until they made it safely through
the gate, where they were greeted by the most
amazing sight. Apple trees and lots of them.
Rows and rows of them standing proud, like
soldiers on parade. Their big red apples shining
in the sunshine. A carpet of red windfall apples
lying beneath them.

Tulip turned to Honey and her sisters and punched her right wing high up in the air.

"Hoorah! We did it! Well done, ladies!"

Her sisters joined her in a little happy dance, which mainly involved them going around and around in circles flapping their wings, happily clucking to each other before falling over laughing because they had made themselves dizzy. This was such an amusing sight which made Honey chuckle.

Rose was the first to come to her senses. She jumped up and dusted herself off, as the adventure wasn't quite over yet. She was soon followed by Daisy and Tulip. However, they all had to help pull Blossom up, who was still rolling around on the ground, giggling.

As they all stood there smiling at each other, they suddenly became aware of how hungry they were, mainly because Blossom's tummy let out an almighty rumble. Now was the right time to give into temptation and eat some of the windfall apples that had fallen from the trees, as they would only go to waste because they were too bruised for the hoomans to want to eat them.

What an almighty feast

The chickens scattered amongst the trees, happily pecking at the fallen apples, which were now a little bruised and soft. Most hoomans would turn their noses up at the thought of eating such apples, but to a chicken, these were the best apples to eat. The soft, mushy flesh gave way to a whole world of juiciness.

They all feasted on the rewarding red apples with not a care in the world. They all agreed that the effort to get to the orchard had most definitely been worth it.

But hang on a minute, was it Honey's imagination or were the apples on the ground moving? *Maybe the heat of the sun was now getting to her,* she thought. It was certainly proving to be a very hot day. She stared at the apple closest to her. It appeared to be wobbling. As she stared more closely, she became conscious of a vibration in her paws followed by a

rumbling sound. This time it was not Blossom's stomach; it was the farmer's tractor making its way up from the lower orchards to the top orchards, where they all were.

Oh heck! thought Honey. *This really isn't good news at all.* She needed to round up her friends and get them to safety quickly.

"Tulip, Rose, Daisy, Blossom, come quickly. The farmer and his tractor are heading our way. We must go now!" shouted Honey.

Tulip, Rose and Daisy came rushing towards her, nervously clucking as they did so. But Blossom was nowhere to be seen. Where was Blossom? The chickens and Honey frantically looked around the nearest trees and began to call for her.

"Blossom! BLOSSOM! Where are you?"

What is all the commotion, thought Blossom, as she stirred from the little nap she had decided to

take. She had eaten
a lot of apples very
quickly and thought
if she took a little
rest and allowed her
tummy to digest them
all, she may then have
room for some more.
She had spotted a wooden
crate full of apples which
had been picked for hooman
consumption. She couldn't think
of a better place to take a nap than amongst
the reddest, most perfectly shaped apples you
had ever seen. She hadn't even considered telling
the others what she had planned to do. Now
listening to her sisters and Honey panicking and
shouting her name, she was starting to think that
this wasn't the greatest idea she had ever had.

"I'm in here!" she called back, frantically
flapping her wings so they could see her.

Honey and the chickens started to run towards
the crate, but the vibrations were getting bigger,
and the noise of the tractor was getting louder

and louder. They looked over their shoulders and saw that the tractor was rapidly approaching them. They had no choice but to dive for cover, as they could not risk being seen.

"Blossom, hide. Don't let the farmer see you!" shouted Tulip. Blossom didn't need telling twice. She pushed down into the apples, out of sight.

The tractor continued to chug and rumble past Honey and the chickens' hiding spot. The noise was deafening to their little ears. Daisy started to cry; she felt scared and was really worried about Blossom. Honey cuddled Daisy to try and reassure her that everything would be OK, and she kept her paws crossed just to be sure.

The farmer was in his own little world, whistling a happy tune as he steered the tractor towards the crate, totally oblivious to Blossom, who was hiding in it. Honey and the chickens all looked on in horror as the farmer lowered the forklift on the front of the tractor and scooped the crate up.

With their mouths wide open, they watched the tractor carrying the crate high up on the forklift start to head towards the farm.

"Whatever are we going to do? How can we rescue poor Blossom?" asked Rose, looking at Honey and her sisters' faces for an answer she didn't currently have. She usually relied on others to guide her in times of trouble. At that moment, a big friendly black and white furry face appeared beside them.

"What appears to be the problem, ladies? Are you in need of assistance?"

It was Major, the farmer's sheepdog and Honey's friend. He was enjoying his moment of freedom, exploring the orchards before being called upon by his master. Honey began to explain the nightmare unravelling in front of them and their urgent need for a plan to rescue Blossom. Major listened carefully. He now understood why they all looked so worried and concerned. He knew he needed to devise a plan, especially as this was his farm, and he knew every inch of it, like the back of his paw. So he pondered for a moment before declaring, "I have it. The perfect rescue plan!"

They all huddled around him, listening intently whilst he told them about his cunning idea to distract the farmer, allowing Blossom to make her escape. If the plan proved successful, no one would even know that Blossom had ever been trapped in the crate. Well, not unless they looked very closely at the apple that Blossom had nervously pecked at because she always eats when she feels anxious.

The great rescue plan

The plan was simple. Tulip, Rose and Daisy were to remain out of sight until called upon. Honey, on the other hand, had to help distract the farmer.

Honey had listened very carefully to Major's plan and now knew what she needed to do to help rescue her friend. She took a big stretch to limber up and, without further hesitation, sprinted off after the tractor like a lion chasing its prey. As she got closer and closer, the realisation that everyone was relying on her began to take its toll. She became very aware of a deafening, thumping sound. It was overpowering all the other sounds around her, even the sound of the tractor appeared to be less obvious. She looked nervously around her to see what it could be. But other than the tractor, there was no other machinery in sight. As she began to focus on the tracks being left by the tractor in the mud, it suddenly hit her, it was coming from inside her.

Her heart was thumping loudly in her chest, the adrenalin of the sprint making the sound amplify more. She took a deep breath and continued to chase after the tractor.

The enormous wheels were now in touching distance, so she darted around the left side of the tractor and across the front of its path. The front wheel narrowly missed her. The plan was incredibly risky, but if she kept her wits about her, she wouldn't be harmed. *Remain focused,* she told herself. Her heart was now attempting to burst through her chest; it was beating so quickly!

The farmer slammed his foot hard down on the brake. Had he imagined it, or had a dog just run across his path? Sure enough, there it was. It was a dog, and it was running around his tractor, making him feel dizzy as he watched it. Clearly, the dog was lost, as no owner was in sight. He couldn't risk moving the tractor and possibly hurting the dog, should it cross his path again. So there was only one thing for it. He had to get

down from the tractor and try to catch it so he could return it to its owner.

As the farmer jumped down from his seat and walked towards her, he began to gently call for her to come to him. Honey stood still, allowing him to get a little closer. When he was in reaching distance, she started to back away, encouraging him to chase her. The plan was working. The farmer was actually chasing after her.

Whilst the chase was on, Major and the chickens ran to the crate and called to Blossom.

"BLOSSOM! QUICK! Jump down from the crate!" shouted Tulip.

Blossom peered over the side of the crate and nervously looked down at the ground below her. She was towering above her sisters and felt scared, but she knew she had no choice but to jump. Some may say she awkwardly fell from the crate, but from this day forth, she would describe it as gently fluttering to the ground, as gracefully as she could, under the circumstances. She landed with a big thump causing a cloud of dust to shoot up from the dry mud, smothering her as it did so. As she began to cough and splutter in the dust, she was pushed to her feet by Major's nose.

"This is not the time to
bathe in the mud, Blossom.
Save that for another day.
You need to get going before
my master sees you all,"
laughed Major.

All four chickens looked at
each other before turning to
look at Major, hoping he would
now lead the way. Major knew what
to do. He ran towards the nearest line of bushes,
calling for them to follow, and they immediately
did so. Just like commando soldiers, they crawled
through the bushes that ran alongside the
orchards, totally camouflaged from any passers-
by. As they reached the end, Honey suddenly
burst through the bush behind them—hot, sweaty
and panting incredibly loudly.

"Quick!" She huffed and puffed. "The farmer is
in the lower orchard looking for me. He didn't
notice that I had doubled back and ran the
opposite way. We just have enough time to run

to the church before he gives up looking for me and returns to his tractor."

Major's rescue plan had been a huge success. So he wished them all good luck before trotting off to locate his poor master, who would be very hot and bothered from searching for a dog that was now no longer in the orchard. No doubt his master would need one of his home-brewed glasses of cold cider when he returned to the farm. It would be well deserved, too, especially after being so unwittingly tricked by his own dog.

Time to go home

Much to their relief, the church gate was in sight. They all ran towards it and continued until they reached the safety of the yew bush. They didn't care now that they may be seen. They just wanted to get home. In the shade of the yew bush, the chickens hugged each other tightly, relieved they were all together again. Honey lay sprawled out next to them, trying hard to get her panting under control. She suddenly felt incredibly tired after exerting so much energy. She just needed to muster up enough strength to help the chickens get back to their coop. Honey began to fixate on the cool water waiting for her in her drinking bowl. She was thirsty and so desperately wanted to get home now.

"Come on, ladies, it is time to go home," she softly muttered.

The chickens all nodded in agreement. They, too, were ready to return to the comfort of their coop. Rose was first to hop over the wall, followed by Daisy, Tulip, Honey and then a very weary Blossom. They scanned their neighbour's garden. The coast was clear, so there was no need to run this time. They slowly walked across the garden to the gap under the fence.

Blossom chose to go first, keeping everything crossed that she wouldn't get stuck this time. Whether it was pure luck or the fact she had burnt off all that she had eaten that day, who knows, but she was able to wiggle herself through the gap to the other side without any assistance from Honey. She smiled to herself, pleased that the coop was now in plain sight. Daisy appeared by her side, as did Rose and Tulip. Honey landed with a gentle thump next to them.

"Well, ladies, the adventure is now over. And what an adventure it was," declared Tulip.

As the chickens excitedly clucked their way back into their coop, Tulip suddenly turned to Honey and, with a huge grin, said, "Thank you for being such a good friend. So until next time, Honey, take care, as I have so many more exciting adventures planned for us all!" And before anything more could be said, she had turned away and was now in the coop with her sisters bickering over who would drink from the water bowl first.

Honey groaned in disbelief but was thankful she was back in her beloved garden, for now at least. She would wait until another day before daring to ask just how involved she would be in these plans.

Honey began to trot down the garden to where her hooman still sat fast asleep. *Oh dear,* she thought. *He looks like the colour of a strawberry. Maybe it is time to wake him up.* So she gently nudged his arm with her little wet nose.

"Oh, hello there, my little honey bear. I must've dozed off for a moment or two. Oh my, hasn't it got hot. We better go inside for a nice cool drink."

Honey barked happily in agreement, so they both toddled off into the kitchen for that well-deserved drink.

About the Author

Honey and The Chickens, The Orchard Escapade, is L J Glasgow's debut book. It was initially written during the second lockdown in 2021 for her own amusement whilst the males in her household were glued to their gaming consoles. The story allowed her to go on a daring imaginary adventure when all were forbidden to do so in the real world. In July 2022, she was encouraged to share the story of this unusual group of friends with others.

L J Glasgow is happiest in her walking boots, with her family and their cockapoo, enjoying the beautiful countryside surrounding where they live in Kent.

Instagram: @ljglasgowauthor
Facebook: @LJGlasgowAuthor

About the Illustrator

Lisa Williams has been illustrating children's books for over 25 years. Inspired by the wide variety of TAUK Kids' projects, she loves helping authors bring their stories to life.

Lisa has developed a wide array of styles as she is always happy to adapt her technique to reflect what instinctively feels 'right' for each project.

Facebook: @lisawilliamsillustration

Acknowledgements

To my friend Vicki Carmichael, who read my early draft. You gave me feedback and the confidence to share this story with others. I will always be truly grateful for that.

I would also like to extend my gratitude to TAUK Publishing and Michelle Catanach. This amazing team has helped me transform a dream into reality. I especially wish to acknowledge Estelle Maher for all the help, support, and guidance you gave me throughout the whole publishing process.

Lisa Williams, I can't thank you enough for bringing my characters to life. The illustrations are fantastic and are so much more than I could have hoped for.

To my parents and my extended family, who have been incredibly supportive throughout this journey.

To my sons, Dominic and William, who have cheered me on and encouraged me to make this something more than just words in a notepad.

And finally, James, you have always been so patient with me, and none of this would have been possible without your love, advice, and support. Thank you!

TAUK
Publishing

TAUK Publishing is an established assisted publisher for independent authors in the UK.

With over 200 titles including novels, non-fiction and children's books, TAUK Publishing is a collaborative-based team providing step-by-step guidance for authors of all genres and formats.

To sign-up to our newsletter or submit an enquiry, visit:

https://taukpublishing.co.uk/contact/

For a one-to-one advice, consider scheduling a Book Clinic:
https://taukpublishing.co.uk/book-clinic/

Connect with us!

Facebook: @TAUKPublishing
Twitter:@TeamAuthorUK
Instagram:@TAUKPublishing
Pinterest:@TeamAuthorUK

We love to hear from new or established authors wanting support in navigating the world of self-publishing. Visit our website for more details on ways we can help you.

https://taukpublishing.co.uk/

SCAN ME